THE CHOCOLATE CHIP MYSTERY

The Chocolate Chip Mystery

By John McInnes

Drawings by Paul Frame

GARRARD PUBLISHING COMPANY
CHAMPAIGN, ILLINOIS

The Chocolate Chip Mystery

Peppino had a job after school.
He helped Max
in his ice cream store.
Peppino helped Max
serve the customers.
He helped Max clean the store.
Sometimes he helped Max
count the money.

Peppino also helped Max
to take care of his dog.
Every afternoon
Peppino took the dog
for a walk.
He was the biggest dog
on the block.
All the children knew him.

He had a name once,
but nobody remembered it.
Everybody called him Fat Dog.
The children loved him.
They gave him candy.
They gave him sandwiches
left over from their lunch bags.
At the ice cream store,
they let him finish
their cones and sundaes.

Fat Dog ate more ice cream
than anyone in the neighborhood.
And, of course,
he got fatter and fatter.
One afternoon Max asked Peppino,
"Will you help me
with something else today?"
"Sure," said Peppino.
"What is it?"
"I want you to taste
these two new ice cream flavors
that I've just made up."
"Why don't you taste them?"
Peppino asked.
"I see so much ice cream,
I've lost my taste for it,"
Max replied.

"Don't you like any flavor?"
Peppino asked.
Max thought and then he said,
"Well, I guess I like
chocolate chip the best.
But I hardly ever eat any."
He handed a dish to Peppino.
It was full of green ice cream.
"Here, try this flavor first,"
he said.
"It's called cucumber ripple."
Peppino tasted it.
"Ugh! It's awful!" he said.
"You don't like it?" Max asked.
"Well, give the rest to Fat Dog.
He likes any kind of ice cream."
Peppino put the bowl on the floor.

Fat Dog came over and tasted it.
Then Fat Dog howled.
He fell on the floor,
rolled over, and played dead.
"Wow," Max said,
"cucumber ripple must be awful
if Fat Dog won't eat it!"

He gave Peppino another dish.
This time it was full
of yellow ice cream.
"Try this one," he said.
"It's called banana cupcake."
Peppino tasted it.
"Mmmm," he said.
"This is really good!"
Peppino gave some to Fat Dog.
Fat Dog liked it
and ate it all.
He wagged his tail.
"You both like banana cupcake,
so I'll make it
my flavor of the week."
Max made a sign
and put it in his store window.

The sign said:

THIS WEEK'S SPECIAL FLAVOR

IS BANANA CUPCAKE—

ONLY AT MAX'S!

Max was looking at his sign
when Mr. Roberts, the postman,
came to the store.
"Hello, Max," he said.

"I'll give you a letter
if you'll make me
a banana cupcake sundae."
Max answered,
"Sure, Mr. Roberts.
I just hope the letter
has good news."
After Max had given
the sundae to Mr. Roberts,
he opened the letter
and read it.
"Oh, no!" Max said.
"What's wrong?" Peppino asked.
Max said sadly,
"This letter says
that the owners
are going to tear down this store."

"But why?"
Peppino asked.
"They're going to tear down
the whole block.
They're going to build
a big office building,"
Max replied.
"That's too bad, Max.
Can't you find another store
that you could rent?"
Mr. Roberts asked.
Max shook his head.
"Not around here," he said.
"I guess I'll have to move away."
"But Max," Peppino cried,
"this is the only
ice cream store for miles.

My friends won't be able
to buy ice cream after school.
And what about Fat Dog?
Who will feed him ice cream?
Who will take him for walks?
I can't if you move away."
Max answered,
"I know, Peppino.

Fat Dog will be sad
to lose his friends,
and so will I.
What else can I do?"
Mr. Roberts finished his sundae.
He put the dish on the floor
for Fat Dog to lick.
"You know, Max," he said,
"there is one store for rent.

I go by it every day."

"Where is it?" Max asked.

Mr. Roberts answered,

"It's around the corner

on the next block.

Come and see it."

Max locked the door.

He and Peppino went
with Mr. Roberts
to see the store.
"There it is,"
said Mr. Roberts.
Max looked at the store.
"I can't rent that place,"
he shouted at Mr. Roberts.

"That's the old Gravely store!"

"Why not?" Peppino asked.

"Because it's haunted,

that's why!" Max answered.

Peppino looked at the store.

It did look spooky.

The windows were dirty.

One of them was boarded up.

There was an old sign
hanging by one nail
on the front door.
It said:
STORE FOR RENT.
APPLY MR. GRAVELY
PHONE 555–2368.
Mr. Roberts said,
"This store isn't haunted.
It hasn't been used
for a long time.
That's why it looks spooky."
Max said,
"I've heard that it's haunted!
Who wants to rent
a haunted store?
No one will buy my ice cream."

Peppino cleaned some dirt
off the window.
He looked into the store.
"It's got a lot of room,"
Peppino said.
"It's much bigger than the store
you have now, Max."

Mr. Roberts said,

"If you painted it

and fixed it up,

it would look very nice."

Max began to think it over.

"Well, I don't know . . . ," he said.

Peppino asked,

"Why don't you call Mr. Gravely

and look at the inside?"

"Okay, I'll call Mr. Gravely.

I'll look at it tomorrow."

The next afternoon,

Peppino went into Max's store.

"Did you call Mr. Gravely?"

he asked.

Max answered,

"Yes, he's waiting for us now."

Max and Peppino and Fat Dog
walked to Mr. Gravely's store.
When they got there,
no one was waiting
to let them in.
"That's funny," Max said.
"He said he would be here."
"Maybe he's inside.
Let's knock,"
Peppino replied.
Max knocked on the door.
From inside they could hear
a thin, old voice.
It said, "Go away!
Can't you see this store is closed?"
Max shouted through the door,
"Mr. Gravely, it's Max.

I've come to see the store.
I may want to rent it."
The old voice said,
"Well, all right, come in."
They opened the door.
Max and Peppino and Fat Dog
stepped into the dark store.
There, in the back of the room,
stood Mr. Gravely.

Peppino felt afraid
when he saw him.
Mr. Gravely was tall and thin.
His face was long and narrow.
He was wearing a black suit
and a tall black hat.
He pointed a thin finger
at Fat Dog.
"I don't let dogs in my store,"
he said in his thin voice.
"Fat Dog won't make any trouble.
He stays in my store,"
Max said.
Then Mr. Gravely replied,
"Very well, he may stay.
But you can see
that I've got my eye on him."

Peppino said,
"It's dark in here.
Aren't there any lights?"
"I think there's one light
that still works.
I'll turn it on,"
Mr. Gravely said.

He pushed a switch,
and one dim light came on.
"Max," Peppino cried,
"it looks like it used to be
an ice cream store!"
In the dim light, they saw
a counter with stools.

Behind it, on the wall,
was a dirty old mirror.
In the middle of the store
there were tables and chairs.
A long time ago
they had been painted red.
Now they were covered with dirt.
Mr. Gravely said,
"It was an ice cream store
a long time ago.
My uncle owned it.
But he had to give it up."
"Why?" Max asked.
Mr. Gravely chuckled.
"Funny things kept
happening to him,"
he said.

"What kind of things?"
Peppino asked.
Mr. Gravely chuckled again.
"Oh, just things," he said.
Just then they heard
a loud crash behind them.
Both Peppino and Max
jumped high in the air.

Max cried,

"What was that?"

Mr. Gravely hadn't jumped at all.

He said calmly, "It was that dog.

I told you he would make trouble.

He knocked over a chair."

"Fat Dog, come here!"

Max called.

"You're supposed to be good,
not scare us to death!"
Mr. Gravely smiled his thin smile.
"Would you like to see
the apartment upstairs?"
he asked.
Max looked surprised.
"Do you rent the apartment
with the store?"
"Yes," Mr. Gravely answered,
"but it hasn't been lived in
since my uncle left."
They climbed the stairs.
One of the steps
made a loud, creaking noise.
The apartment was dusty and dirty.
Peppino looked around.

"It needs fixing up," he said.
"But it's not bad.
You and Fat Dog
could live here, Max."
Mr. Gravely rubbed his hands.
"It would save you money too.
You could live and work
in the same place."

Max turned to Mr. Gravely.
"I'd like to know
about those things
that happened to your uncle."
Mr. Gravely said,
"Oh, I'm quite sure
they won't happen to you."
Max looked around.

"The store isn't haunted?"
he asked.
"Haunted?" Mr. Gravely said.
"What an idea!
You don't believe in ghosts,
do you?"
"Well, no . . . ," Max said.
He looked around again.
"Okay, Mr. Gravely," he said,
"I'd like to rent it."
They agreed on the price.
Max painted the store
inside and out.
Peppino washed the mirror
behind the counter.
They painted the tables
and chairs a bright pink.

They cleaned the rooms upstairs.
A month later, Max and Fat Dog
moved into the new store.
Max had a big new sign made
to hang outside the store.
It said:

THIS IS MAX'S

NEW ICE CREAM STORE.

He made another sign
for the window.
It said:

IT'S A NEW STORE, FOLKS!

BUT MAX'S ICE CREAM

IS STILL THE SAME—DELICIOUS!

When Peppino came to work
on the first day,
there weren't any people
in the store.
"It'll take a while
for everyone to know I've moved,"
Max said.
But a week went by
and still very few people
came to the new store.
Max was worried.

"Maybe I should not
have moved in here,"
he said.
"People may still think
that the store is haunted.
They may be right.
Something funny is going on."
Peppino was surprised.
"Max, what do you mean?"
he asked.
Max looked at Peppino.
"I want you to keep
this a secret," he said.
"I've got a mystery
on my hands.
My ice cream is disappearing."
"Disappearing?" Peppino cried.

"Where does it go?"

Max shook his head.

"I don't know," he said.

"Every morning when I come down,
more ice cream is gone.
What's even more strange—
it's always chocolate chip."

"Maybe Fat Dog takes it,"
Peppino said.

"He's been getting fatter lately."

Max shook his head.

"No, it can't be Fat Dog.
He always sleeps in my room.
And I keep the door closed."

Peppino thought about it.

"This really is a mystery,"
he said.

Peppino went into the store
the next afternoon.
"Did any more ice cream
disappear last night?" he asked.
"Yes, it did," Max replied.
"It was chocolate chip."
Then Peppino had an idea.

"Max," he said,

"let me sleep in the store tonight.

It's Friday, and I think

my parents will let me.

I can bring my sleeping bag."

Max thought for a while.

"I don't know," he said.

"It might be dangerous."

"Oh, no," said Peppino.

"You're upstairs if I need you."

Max thought about it.

Then he said, "Okay, Peppino,

if your parents will let you."

Peppino's parents said that

he could stay in the store.

Peppino went back to the store

with his sleeping bag.

When closing time came,
Max and Peppino
went upstairs for dinner.
Max did not eat much dinner.
"Why aren't you eating?"
Peppino asked.
"I don't know.
That's another mystery.

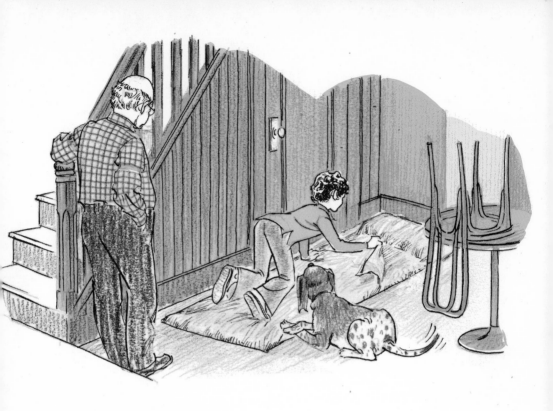

Lately I haven't been hungry,"
Max answered.
"Boy," Peppino said,
"things are really strange
around here!"
When it was time for bed,
Peppino put his sleeping bag
on the floor of the store.

Max gave him a flashlight
to put beside his pillow.
"You go up to bed,"
Peppino said bravely to Max.
"I'll keep watch down here."
Max said,
"Okay, but Fat Dog
will stay with you.

If you hear anything,
yell for me."
"I will," Peppino said.
Max said good night to Peppino
and to Fat Dog.
Then he went upstairs.
Peppino was alone
in the dark store.

He stayed awake for the first hour.

Nothing happened.

Then, as time passed,

Peppino got very sleepy.

"I'll just close my eyes

for a minute," he thought.

Soon he was sound asleep.

Late at night

a noise awakened Peppino.

He raised his head and listened.

Peppino felt afraid.

The noise sounded like

the creaking stair step.

He tried to see into the dark.

A white shape was coming downstairs.

"Yeow! It's a ghost!"

Peppino thought to himself.

He was too frightened to move.
The ghost shape
went behind the counter.
Peppino heard another noise.
The ice cream freezer
was being opened.
That noise awakened Fat Dog.
He ran across the store
and behind the counter.

Peppino turned on his flashlight.
He thought he saw a ghost
behind the counter.
But it wasn't a ghost.
It was Max
in a long, white night shirt.
He was putting ice cream
into two big dishes.

It was chocolate chip ice cream!
Max put one dish on the floor
for Fat Dog.
Then he started to eat
from the other dish.
"Max, what are you doing?"
Peppino whispered.
Max didn't answer.

He went on eating the ice cream.
Peppino turned the flashlight
on Max's face.
Peppino saw that
his eyes were closed.
Max was sound asleep!
"So Max is the ghost,"
Peppino said to himself.

"He's a sleepwalking,
ice cream eating ghost!"
Peppino went behind the counter.
He shook Max's arm.
Max woke up.
"What is it?" Max cried.
"What's wrong?
Did you find the ghost?"
Peppino laughed.
"I sure did," he answered.
"Where? How? When?" Max asked.
Then he looked around.
"Where am I?
Why is this ice cream here?"
"You've been eating
chocolate chip ice cream
every night," Peppino said.

Max looked surprised.

"You mean I've been sleepwalking?"
he asked.

"Yes," Peppino said,

"and sleep eating too.

You were asleep when

you came down those steps!"

Just then Fat Dog finished
his bowl of ice cream.
He lifted his head
and sniffed Max's bowl.
Then he stood on his back legs
and ate the rest
of Max's ice cream.

"I can see why Fat Dog
is getting fatter too,"
Max said.
"From now on,
I'll have a small dish
of chocolate chip ice cream
before I go to bed.

That should keep me
from walking in my sleep."
Peppino took his sleeping bag
up to Max's room.
They went back to sleep.
The mystery had been solved.
The next morning, Max said,
"You've solved one problem,
Peppino, but I still have another.

I don't have any customers."
Peppino thought for a minute.
"Max," he said,
"you feel that everyone thinks
that this store is haunted, right?"
"Right!" Max answered.
"That's bad for business."
"Maybe we could make it
good for business," Peppino said.
He told Max his idea.
"Great!" Max cried.
"Let's give it a try!"
That day Max ordered
a new sign
for the store.
It said:
MAX'S HAUNTED ICE CREAM STORE.

He put another sign
in the window:
THIS WEEK'S FLAVOR
IS GHOST AND GINGERSNAP.
IT'S SURE TO SEND SHIVERS
UP YOUR SPINE!

Max and Peppino bought
paper ghosts, witches, and bats
and put them in the store.
It looked like Halloween
when they were finished.
Both Max and Peppino put on
ghost costumes when they worked
behind the counter.

Max thought of a new sundae.
It was called the goblin special.
It was made with orange ice
and chocolate sauce.
Peppino and Fat Dog loved it,
so Max knew it was good.
All of Max's customers
started to come into the new store.

The children on the street
loved the new goblin special too.
Soon Max was busier
than he had ever been.
One day Max and Peppino
were hard at work.
A customer asked,
"Hey, Max, don't you eat
your own ice cream?"
Max smiled at Peppino.
"I hate ice cream," he said,
"but I do eat a small dish
of chocolate chip every night.
It helps me to sleep!"